Rodeo Kids

Written and Illustrated by Norah Kersh

Dedicated to Lane Frost, Blake Hallam, Damon McCoy, Matthew Kersh, and all the men and women who've gone to the great Rodeo in the sky.

Published by:
Boolarong Press
38/1631 Wynnum Road
Tingalpa Qld 4173
Australia.
www.boolarongpress.com.au

Graphics and layout by Rosana Kersh

First published 2019

A catalogue record for this book is available from the National Library of Australia

ISBN: 9781925877281 (paperback)

Printed and bound by Watson Ferguson & Company, Tingalpa, Australia

A Cowboys prayer

Our Gracious and Heavenly Father,

We pause in the midst of this festive occasion, mindful and thoughtful of the guidance that you have given us. We would ask today, Lord, that you be with us in this rodeo arena as we pray you will be also with us in life's arena. As cowboys, Lord, we don't ask for any special favours in this arena today. We only ask that you will let us compete in this event, and in life, as You did for us. We don't ask that we never break a barrier, draw the steer that won't lay, draw around a chute fighting horse, or a bull that is impossible to ride. Help us to compete in life as honest as the horse we ride; in a manner as clean and pure as the wind that blows across this Australian country; so when we make that Last Ride, that we know is inevitable, to the Country Up There…where the grass is green and lush and stirrup-high and the water runs clean and clear…You will tell us, as our Last Judge, that our entry fees are paid. Amen.

Tillie, Jack and Ruby are coming in from the station because...
The Rodeo is on today. The kids have been counting the days.

Mum and Dad meet with neighbours and friends.
Tillie, Jack and Ruby see School of the Air friends.
They see fairy floss and fancy belts and shirts.
What can they buy?

In the yards behind the chutes, broncs, bulls and steers mill about. They have come a long way in big trucks. There is Dakota pushing bulls through the gate. To her they are cherished pets. But wait...

On the flat, near the creek are the competitors camps.

Some are warming up their horses.

The rodeo is about to begin.

With flags held high, riders canter around the arena and line up, hats off for Advance Australia Fair.
They say the Cowboy's Prayer asking God's protection for competitors and animals.

The fun begins. It is the Poddy Calf ride.

Some kids stick like burrs.

Others tumble in the dust.

Next....

See the Barrel racer go. Light on the reins, this girl and her horse are quick around the barrels and it's a fast run home. The crowd cheers.

Now for Team roping. Like a bolt of lightning out runs the steer. Darcy's rope loops the horns...
Jace twirls his rope towards those flying heels.
It's a catch! How is the time?

Next event is Steer wrestling.
Tate dives from his horse, grips the scary horns. Oh-Oh! That steer is too fast, drags this man in the dust and gets away.
Well, better luck next time?

Clang! The gate opens,
Out dashes the calf.
Dirt and dust. Rope and tie.
The job is done.

Who wants to get on a bull called Thunder and Light?
Rampage or Chainsaw?
Yay! The bullriders do!
The music pounds, the bull spins, thumping and bumping.
Will that cowboy make eight seconds?
Oh no! He is gone. Flung flat on the dirt.
The bull kicks up dust. Angry.

The clown rushes in, get that bull distracted.
Suddenly Rampage turns and chases the clown.

Slowly, the bull rider gets up and limps away.
Good to go another round.

The children play on the mechanical bull,

"It looks pretty easy," says Tillie.

It is NOT so easy.

They decide to practise on the poddies back home.

As the sun goes down, they must say goodbye to their friends,
for it is a long drive home.
First thing tomorrow the weaners in the yard must be fed.

The End.

MORE BOOKS BY NORAH KERSH

Outback Alphabet-Boolarong Press
Outback Countout-Boolarong Press
Grandma's Precious Chest-Boolarong Press
Bushfire-Boolarong Press

The Sugar Bag Baby-Self published
The Poddy Calf-Self published
Rush -Self published
Dry Grass Whispering (Autobiography)-Self published
The Etta Plains Story (Biography)-Self published
Gulf Women (Mixed authors)

Eggs Don't Come From Cartons-Self published
Then Mummy Went to Bed-Self published
Outback Doctor-Boolarong Press
Outback Songs-Boolarong Press
(Illustrations only)